ASTERIX
AND CLEOPATRA

TEXT BY GOSCINNY

DRAWINGS BY UDERZO

TRANSLATED BY ROBERT STEVEN CARON

DARGAUD PUBLISHING INTERNATIONAL, LTD.

ISBN 0-917201-75-2

Exclusive licenced distributor for USA:

Distribooks Inc.
8220 N. Christiana Ave.
Skokie, IL 60076-2911
Tel: (708) 676-1596
Fax: (708) 676-1195
Toll-free fax: 800-433-9229

Imprimé en France-Publiphotoffset 93500 Pantin-en mars 1995

Printed in France

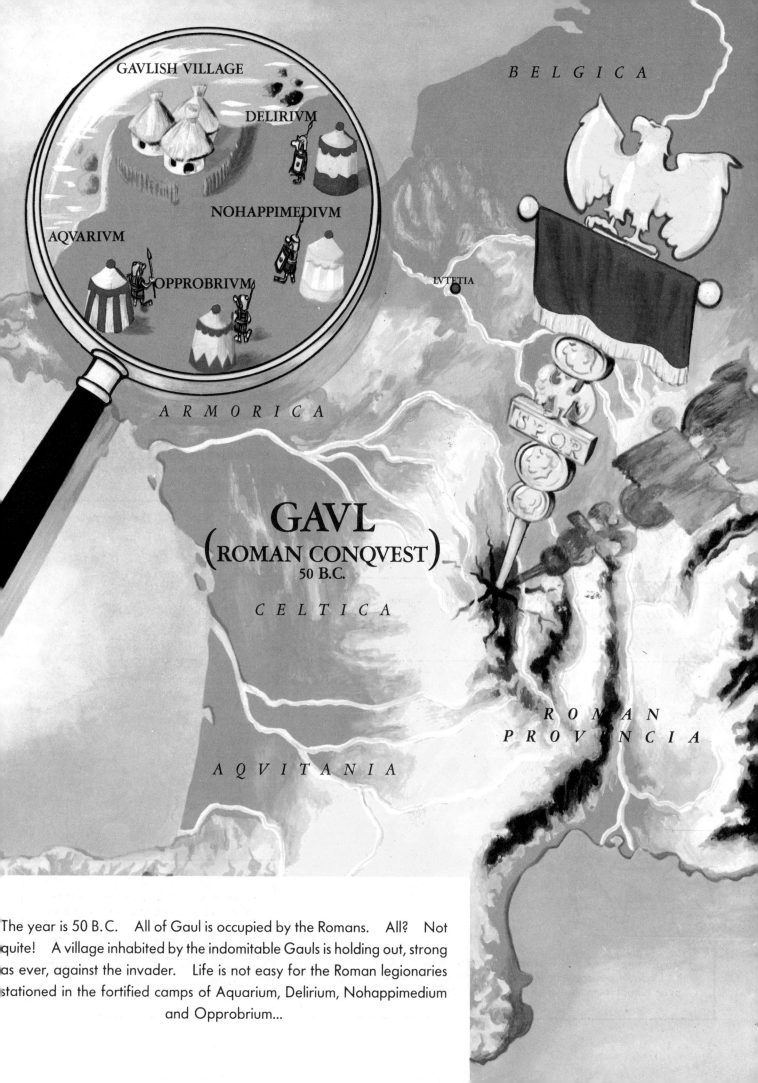

GAVLISH VILLAGE

DELIRIVM

NOHAPPIMEDIVM

AQVARIVM

OPPROBRIVM

ARMORICA

GAVL
(ROMAN CONQVEST)
50 B.C.

CELTICA

AQVITANIA

BELGICA

LVTETIA

ROMAN PROVINCIA

The year is 50 B.C. All of Gaul is occupied by the Romans. All? Not quite! A village inhabited by the indomitable Gauls is holding out, strong as ever, against the invader. Life is not easy for the Roman legionaries stationed in the fortified camps of Aquarium, Delirium, Nohappimedium and Opprobrium...

A FEW GAULS...

The hero of these adventures is Asterix. He is a cunning, quick-witted little warrior, so all the dangerous missions are automatically entrusted to him. Asterix owes his superhuman strength to the magic potion brewed by the Druid, Magigimmix...

Obelix is the side-kick of Asterix. He is a menhir delivery-man by trade, and relishes wild boar. Obelix is always ready to drop everything order to seek new adventures with Asterix... as long as the wild boar is plentiful and the fighting is rough...

Magigimmix, the venerable village druid, gathers mistletoe and concocts magic potions. His greatest discovery is the potion that confers superhuman strength on all who imbibe it. But Magigimmix has other recipes up his sleeve...

Finally, there is Macroeconomix, chief of the tribe. This majestic, courageous and touchy old warrior is respected by his men and feared by his enemies. Macroeconomix has just one fear – that the sky may fall on his head. But as he himself would say, "Fat chance!"

Malacoustix is the bard. Opinion is divided as to his talent. He thinks it is laudable, but everyone else finds it deplorable. However, as long as he keeps his mouth shut he is a jolly companion esteemed by all...

ALEXANDRIA, CAPITAL OF THE KINGDOM OF EGYPT, IN THE PALACE OF THE LEGENDARY QUEEN CLEOPATRA, ABOUT WHOM IT HAS BEEN SAID THAT HAD HER NOSE BEEN SHORTER, THE WHOLE FACE OF THE WORLD WOULD HAVE CHANGED.

THAT'S AN INFAMOUS ASSERTION, O CAESAR!...

YOU HAVE TO FACE FACTS, O QUEEN! YOUR EGYPTIANS ARE A DECADENT PEOPLE, ONLY FIT TO LIVE IN SEMI-SLAVERY UNDER THE ROMANS.

MY PEOPLE BUILT THE PYRAMIDS! THE TOWER OF PHAROS! THE TEMPLES! THE OBELISKS!

THAT'S ANCIENT HISTORY. NOW ALL THEY CAN DO IS WAIT FOR THE NILE FLOODS!...

ENOUGH OF THAT!

CRASH

I SHALL PROVE TO YOU, O CAESAR, THAT MY PEOPLE HAVE NOT LOST THEIR SPARK OF GENIUS! IN THREE MONTHS TO THE DAY, I SHALL HAVE A SPLENDID PALACE BUILT FOR YOU HERE IN ALEXANDRIA!

IF YOU SUCCEED, O QUEEN, I SHALL ADMIT THAT THE EGYPTIANS ARE STILL A GREAT PEOPLE!...

...BUT I DOUBT IT!

SHE'S A SWEETHEART, BUT HER NOSE IS SO EASILY PUT OUT OF JOINT...

CRASH

AND SUCH A PRETTY NOSE IT IS TOO!

SOON AFTERWARDS

NOTE: FOR THE CONVENIENCE OF OUR READERS, WE ARE PROVIDING A DUBBED VERSION OF THE DIALOGUE...

I HAVE SUMMONED YOU, METROPOLIS, BECAUSE YOU ARE THE BEST ARCHITECT IN ALEXANDRIA... WHICH ISN'T SAYING MUCH.

OH!*

* AS DUBBING TECHNIQUES HAD YET TO BE PERFECTED WAY BACK THEN, THE LIP MOVEMENTS MAY NOT BE IN SYNCH WITH THE WORDS.

DON'T TALK BACK! YOUR BUILDINGS ARE FLIMSY! YOU CAN HEAR EVERYTHING THE NEIGHBORS ARE SAYING! THE CEILINGS CAVE IN!

IT'S THOSE NEWFANGLED MATERIALS... BESIDES, WHAT I'D REALLY LIKE TO DO IS BUILD PYRAMIDS AND...

SILENCE! YOU HAVE THREE MONTHS TO MAKE AMENDS BY BUILDING A MAGNIFICENT PALACE HERE IN ALEXANDRIA, FOR JULIUS CAESAR!

DID I HEAR YOU SAY THREE MONTHS?

IF YOU SUCCEED, I'LL COVER YOU WITH GOLD. IF NOT, I'LL THROW YOU TO THE CROCODILES! NOW, GET OUT!

THREE MONTHS!... TO DO THIS JOB, I'LL NEED SUPERNATURAL POWERS!... HELP FROM A WIZARD!

WHY OF COURSE! I KNOW JUST THE MAN I NEED! HE CAN DO WONDERS!

SMACK!

VERY FAR AWAY, IN A LITTLE GAULISH VILLAGE...

CDLVI* AGAIN!... WHAT A BIT OF WIZARDRY!

HEY! HEY! STRAIGHT FROM THE WIZARD!

THAT ROMAN GAME WILL NEVER CATCH ON HERE...

*456

6

THE PEACE THAT PREVAILS IN THE VILLAGE OF INDOMITABLE GAULS IS SOON TO BE DISTURBED...

I'M GOING TO TRAIN THIS LITTLE DOG TO CARRY MENHIRS! ...

SURE. IN THE MEANTIME, TRAIN YOUR EYES ON THIS HEFTY BOAR AND SET THE TABLE.

... BY THE ARRIVAL OF A STRANGE STRANGER ...

CAN YOU TELL ME WHERE TO FIND THE DRUID MAGIGIMMIX?

UP IN THAT TREE, GATHERING MISTLETOE.

MAGIGIMMIX?

OH, WHAT A PLEASANT SURPRISE!

?!

HOW PLEASED I AM, DEAR FRIEND, TO SEE YOU ONCE AGAIN.

AN ALEXANDRINE...

THIS IS MY FRIEND, METROPOLIS, AN ARCHITECT FROM ALEXANDRIA, WHOM I MET DURING MY TRAVELS.

I HAVE MADE THIS LONG JOURNEY, O MAGIGIMMIX, BECAUSE I NEED YOUR HELP.

I MUST BUILD A PALACE FOR CAESAR IN THREE MONTHS OR ELSE CLEOPATRA WILL THROW ME TO THE CROCODILES! ...

... AND WITHOUT YOUR MAGIC POWER, I'LL NEVER MANAGE TO DO IT! BOUHOUHOUHOU!

CAN YOU EAT CROCODILES?

SHH, OBELIX!

CALM DOWN, METROPOLIS. AS A MATTER OF FACT, I WANTED TO LOOK OVER A FEW MANUSCRIPTS IN THE ALEXANDRIAN LIBRARY...

THIS IS A GOOD OPPORTUNITY! I'LL GO BACK TO EGYPT WITH YOU! ...

US TOO!

BY OSIRIS! ARE YOU SERIOUS?

BOW WOW!

3 IV

8

WE CAN CAST OFF NOW, ATYOURSERVIS!

BELIEVE ME, ASTERIX, I HAVE NO IDEA HOW HE GOT INTO MY BAG!...

SURE, SURE! KEEP MOVING OR YOU'LL MAKE US MISS THE TIDE.

AND WITH A BITTER WINTER WIND NIPPING AT THEIR NOSES, OUR FRIENDS EMBARK ON THEIR LONG JOURNEY TO EGYPT.

IN EGYPT WE'LL HAVE TO CONTEND WITH A TIGHT DEADLINE, LABOR PROBLEMS, THE ROMANS, WHO'LL TRY TO STOP US FROM WINNING CLEOPATRA'S BET...

AND ABOVE ALL WITH A RIVAL ARCHITECT NAMED MYNEMESIS, WHO IS ALWAYS TRYING TO DO ME IN... HE HAS MANY TALENTS...

IS HE VERY GIFTED?...

NO, RICH. HE HAS MANY GOLD TALENTS. THAT'S THE CURRENCY IN CIRCULATION IN EGYPT.

AND OF COURSE THERE'S ALWAYS THE THREAT OF PIRATES ON THE HIGH SEAS!

OH, WE CAN HANDLE THAT! RIGHT, OBELIX?

AND INDEED, NOT FAR AWAY...

AYE, MATES, TO GET HOLD OF THIS BOAT, I HAD TO LEAVE MY SON ERIX AS SECURITY. SO, THIS TIME LET'S AVOID THOSE GAULS AND STEER CLEAR OF THE GAULISH, ROMAN AND PHOENICIAN SHIPS THEY NORMALLY USE.

EGYPTIAN SHIP TO STARBOARD

SPLENDID! WE'LL RECOUP OUR LOSSES! MAKE READY TO BOARD HER!

WHAT IS THAT LOOK-OUT SAYING?

HE SAYS THERE'S A PIRATE SHIP TO PORT!

REALLY? YOU'RE NOT PUTTING US ON?!!?

IT'S THEM, ASTERIX! IT'S THEM!... YOOHOO! WE'RE BAAACK!

I CAN'T BELIEVE IT! IT CAN'T BE TRUE! IT'S THEM AGAIN! STIR YOUR STUMPS! LET'S BEAT IT IF THERE'S STILL TIME!

THERE'S NO TIME, CAPTAIN! THEIR STUMPS ARE FASTER THAN OURS!... SO WHAT SHOULD WE DO?

WE'RE STUMPED! SCUTTLE HER! THE PAYOFF WILL BE THE SAME AND WE'LL AVOID A FEW SHINERS...

SOON AFTERWARDS...

WELL, YOU TALKED OF EVERYTHING WE'D HAVE AND NOW WE'VE BEEN HAD. ALEA JACTA EST!..

ONE MORE WORD AND I'LL MAKE YOU EAT YOUR WOODEN STUMP!!!

TWO TIMERS! THAT DOESN'T COUNT! BAD SPORTS!!!

THAT'S AMAZING! THOSE PIRATES JUST SAW YOU AND GAVE UP, THEN THEY SANK THEIR OWN SHIP!

OH, THEY'RE OLD ACQUAINTANCES.. WE OFTEN GO SAILING TOGETHER!

ONE NIGHT, AFTER A LONG, PEACEFUL VOYAGE...

WHAT'S THAT LIGHT ON THE HORIZON, METROPOLIS?

THAT'S THE TOWER OF PHAROS, ASTERIX. ITS LIGHT GUIDES SHIPS INTO THE HARBOR...

WE'LL REACH ALEXANDRIA TOMORROW.

A TOWER TO GUIDE SHIPS? THESE EGYPTIANS ARE CRAZY!

IT'S ONE OF THE SEVEN WONDERS OF THE WORLD, OBELIX!

AS SOON AS WE LAND, I'LL TAKE YOU TO THE PALACE TO MEET THE QUEEN.

IN HER PALACE, THE EXTRAVAGANT CLEOPATRA IS PREPARING TO PARTAKE OF HER FAVORITE SNACK: PEARLS DISSOLVED IN VINEGAR.

WHERE ARE THE PEARL TONGS, FOR OSIRIS'S SAKE?

HERE, TASTER, DO YOUR JOB!

VERY WELL, O QUEEN!

THAT GREEDY LITTLE GORGER HAS PUT IN FOUR PEARLS AGAIN!

UGH! HOW I HATE WHEN SHE OVERDOES THE PEARLS IN VINEGAR!

METROPOLIS, THE ARCHITECT, CRAVES THE HONOR OF AN AUDIENCE!

LET HIM ENTER...

ALLOW ME TO INTRODUCE MY FRIENDS FROM GAUL, O QUEEN — A POWERFUL MAGICIAN AND TWO BRAVE WARRIORS WHO ARE HERE TO HELP ME...

DOGMATIX!

GRRROARRRR!

VERY WELL, BUT MAKE IT SNAPPY! THERE ISN'T MUCH TIME LEFT, AND CAESAR KEEPS PRODDING ME. IF YOU SUCCEED, THERE'LL BE GOLD FOR ONE AND ALL... OTHERWISE, THE CROCODILES!

... AND I'M WARNING YOU, METROPOLIS, YOUR RIVAL, MYNEMESIS, RESENTS THAT I CHOSE YOU OVER HIM TO BUILD CAESAR'S PALACE. NOTHING WOULD PLEASE HIM MORE THAN TO SEE YOU SQUIRMING INSIDE A CROCODILE. NOW, BE OFF!

SHE LOOKS LIKE SHE HAS A SHORT FUSE, BUT SHE DOES HAVE A PRETTY NOSE...

A VERY PRETTY NOSE!

11

COME OVER TO MY PLACE!

THIS IS YOUR HOUSE?!...

WHY, YES, I BUILT IT MYSELF!...

THE DOOR'S JAMMED AGAIN... I MUST HAVE MADE A MISTAKE IN THE PLANS...

LET ME GIVE YOU A HAND.

CRASH

NO, OBELIX!

DON'T YELL AT HIM... IT WILL BE MORE FUNCTIONAL LIKE THAT.

POF! POF! POF!

UH... WATCH OUT FOR THE STEPS!

I HAVE THE FEELING YOU REALLY DID NEED OUR HELP, METROPOLIS.

THIS IS WHERE I WORK... ALLOW ME TO INTRODUCE MY SCRIBE, PAPYRIS, WHO IS A FAITHFUL FRIEND. HE HAS AN EXCELLENT COMMAND OF YOUR LANGUAGE AND SPEAKS ALL THE OTHER MODERN LANGUAGES: LATIN, GREEK, CELTIC, ETC...

IS IT A GOOD POSITION BEING A SCRIBE?...

IT'S A JOB YOU CAN TAKE SITTING DOWN, SQUATTING, ACTUALLY!

AND HOW DOES ONE BECOME A SCRIBE?

I TOOK A CORRESPONDENCE COURSE... A VERY GOOD SCHOOL...

THE CATALOGUE SAID ANYONE WHO COULD DRAW COULD WRITE!

DURING THEIR LENTIL*BREAK, THE WORKERS HAVE AN UNEXPECTED VISITOR ...

*A VERY POPULAR EGYPTIAN DISH.

AND THEY QUICKLY GET THE WHOLE PICTURE.

TEEHEEHEE!

AND WHEN THE BREAK IS OVER ...

BOUHOUHOUHOU

... THE WORKERS' WILLINGNESS TO WORK ...

... HAS BEEN BROKEN.

MASTER! THE WORKERS REFUSE TO GET ON WITH THE JOB! I THINK SOMEONE'S TURNED THEM AGAINST YOU!

ALL THESE HEAD-ACHES MAKE MY BLOOD CURDLE, AT THIS RATE, I'LL BE UNFIT FOR CROCODILE CONSUMPTION!

SO' MUCH THE BETTER! WHY MAKE THEM SUCH A GOOD MEAL?

BECAUSE THEY'RE SACRED CROCODILES! YOU CAN'T JUST GIVE THEM ANYONE TO EAT!

THESE EGYPTIANS ARE CRAZY!

LET'S SEE WHAT'S GOING ON!

JUST WHAT I THOUGHT! THEY'RE DEMANDING ANOTHER DECREASE.

YOU MEAN AN INCREASE.

NO, WAGES HAVE NOTHING TO DO WITH IT, THEY'RE VERY WELL PAID. THEY'RE DEMANDING A DECREASE IN WHIPLASHES... BUT IF I DO THAT, THEY WON'T WHIP THROUGH THE TASK AND THE PALACE WILL NEVER BE FINISHED IN TIME!

YOU'RE WHIPPING UP MY ANGER WITH ALL THESE STORIES! THIS IS NO WAY TO TREAT PEOPLE! ASTERIX, LIGHT A GOOD FIRE UNDER THAT CAULDRON!...

NOW LET ME SHOW YOU HOW TO MAKE MEN WORK!...

NO, NOT YOU.

WELL, THANKS A WHOLE LOT.

HOW ABOUT A LITTLE DEMONSTRATION, ASTERIX!

GLOUP! GLOUP! GLOUP!

WOOF! WOOF!

POF!

16

12

17

THESE AMAZING FOREIGN WIZARDS WILL END UP HELPING METROPOLIS TO WIN! I HAVE TO DO SOMETHING!

PROBOSCIS!

WHAT CAN I DO FOR YOU, MYNEMESIS?

I KNOW METROPOLIS IS EXPECTING A CARGO OF STONE THAT IS BEING SHIPPED DOWN THE NILE FROM THE COUNTRY... THAT STONE MUST NEVER REACH THE BUILDING SITE... HERE'S SOME GOLD TO MAKE SURE IT DOESN'T.

PROBOSCIS MEETS THE FLEET CARRYING THE STONE TO THE BUILDING SITE, AND THE GOLD QUICKLY HELPS THE CAPTAIN TO OVERCOME HIS SCRUPLES.

✳ UNLOAD THOSE STONES!

✳ NOT ON THE BANK! ON THE OTHER SIDE!

BONK!

THE WORKERS, WHO ARE FROM RURAL EGYPT, OBEY WITHOUT QUESTION.

SPLASH

SPLOSH!

✳ HAIN'T NO USE FISHIN FOR REASONS OR WE'LL REALLY BE IN A STEW.
✳ IF YA AX ME, DA CAP'N'S ROWIN WIT ONE OAR IN DA WATER

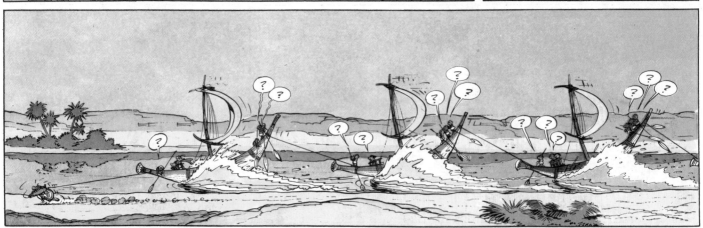

LET'S GO! UP AND AT 'EM YOU SLEEPY HEADS. THE SUN'S UP! WE'RE OFF TO SEE THE SPHINX AND THE PYRAMIDS!

HMMM!... JUST A FEW MORE MINUTES! HMMM...

SOON AFTERWARDS...

SO, WHAT DO YOU THINK? WASN'T IT WORTH THE TRIP?

IT'S AWESOME, BY BELISAMA!

LEAVE IT ALONE, DOGMATIX!

GRRRR

SOUVENIRS

SOUVENIRS

SOUVENIRS

NOBLE TOURIST, HOW ABOUT A SOUVENIR PORTRAIT OF YOURSELF WITH THE SPHINX?

WHY NOT? IT WILL BE A HANDSOME ADDITION TO MY HUT.

WE'LL JUST GO POKE OUR NOSES AROUND.

THAT'S FINE.

NOW STAND SO I CAN SEE YOU IN PROFILE, WITH YOUR SHOULDERS FACING FORWARD, AND DON'T MOVE, PLEASE.

THE VIEW MUST BE SOMETHING FROM UP THERE.

NO, OBELIX! I'M SURE YOU'RE NOT ALLOWED!

THERE HE GOES AGAIN! ASTERIX IS ALWAYS GIVING ORDERS!

!

CRACK!

?

17

21

22

IF THEY EVER GET OUT OF THERE, BY ISIS, I SWEAR I'LL NEVER SHAVE MY HEAD AGAIN!

OKAY. FIRST OF ALL, WE HAVE TO GET THIS DOOR OPEN.

NONE OF THIS WOULD EVER HAVE HAPPENED INSIDE A MENHIR!...

IN VIEW OF THE CIRCUMSTANCES, OBELIX, I'M GOING TO GIVE YOU SOME OF MY MAGIC POTION FOR THE VERY FIRST TIME.

REALLY?

YOU HEARD WHAT THE MAN SAID!

ONE DROP, TWO DROPS, THREE DROPS... THAT SHOULD DO IT.

AND NOW, THIS WAY TO THE EGRESS!

I CAN'T TELL HOW GLAD I AM THAT I CAME INSIDE THE PYRAMID...

WHAM

SWOOSHH!

BUT I DON'T SEE MUCH DIFFERENCE BEFORE AND AFTER THE POTION...

NOW WE'VE GOT TO FIND OUR WAY THROUGH THESE LABYRINTHINE CORRIDORS...

THAT'LL BE THE TOUGHEST JOB OF - ALL...

SURE ENOUGH, SEVERAL HOURS LATER...

THIS IS THE TENTH TIME WE'VE WOUND UP IN THE SAME SPOT... THOSE PHARAOHS SURE HAD GOOD ARCHITECTS.

THIS IS SERIOUS.

VERY SERIOUS, I'M STARTING TO GET HUNGRY.

24

INSIDE THE PYRAMID...

MY POWERS ARE NOT STRONG ENOUGH TO GET US OUT OF HERE... I'M VERY MUCH AFRAID THIS MAY BE THE END OF OUR ADVENTURES, BY BELENOS!

I FEEL SORRY FOR METROPOLIS... WITHOUT US, HE'LL WIND UP INSIDE A CROCODILE.

AND ME, I FEEL SORRY FOR MY POOR LITTLE DOGMATIX... DON'T I, DOGMATIX?

DOGMATIX?

WHY, YES, DOGMATIX! YOU'RE NOT GOING TO TRIM ME DOWN FOR BRINGING HIM? THE FACT IS, I DIDN'T BRING HIM, HE CAME ALL BY HIMSELF!

THAT'S RIGHT! HIS SENSE OF SMELL HAS LED HIM TO US... SO HE CAN FIND HIS WAY BACK AGAIN AND HELP US GET OUT OF HERE!

OF COURSE HE CAN!

DOGMATIX, IF YOU HELP US GET OUT OF HERE, YOU'LL GET A HUGE BONE OUTSIDE!

YOU'LL GET TWO HUGE BONES!

HEAPS OF HUGE BONES!

I APOLOGIZE, OBELIX. YOU WERE QUITE RIGHT TO BRING YOUR POOCHY!

SOMETIMES I GET THE FEELING HE UNDERSTANDS EVERYTHING I SAY!

AFTER A VOYAGE OF MANY STADIA*...

MY FRIENDS ARE BACK AT LAST!

AND WE'VE BROUGHT YOU ENOUGH STONE TO FINISH THE PALACE!

*AN CIENT ROMAN UNIT OF LENGTH OF ABOUT 184 METERS. AS THERE ARE 30.48 METERS IN A FOOT AND 12 FEET IN AN ALEXANDRINE, IT IS EASY TO COMPUTE THAT THERE ARE AROUND 50½ ALEXANDRINES IN ONE STADIUM.

THE WORKERS, HAVING DOWNED THEIR DOSE OF MAGIC POTION, WORK FEVERISHLY.

IF I WASN'T HERE TO CORRECT THESE PLANS!...

I'VE JUST LEARNED THAT CLEOPATRA'S COMING TO VISIT THE WORKSITE!

AND SO IT IS...

NO NEED TO STOP. I'M JUST PAYING A LITTLE INFORMAL VISIT, IN COGNITO... PLEASE, CARRY ON.

THERE'S NO DOUBT ABOUT IT, SHE DOES HAVE A PRETTY NOSE!

A VERY PRETTY NOSE!

DID YOU SEE HER NOSE DOGMATIX?

MEANWHILE, IN MYNEMESIS'S HOUSE.

AN IDEA! I NEED AN IDEA!

HELP ME! AND FOR THE LAST TIME, GO AND SHAVE YOUR HEAD!!!

I CAN'T, MASTER. I MADE A VOW...

I THINK I'VE GOT IT, SHE'LL HAVE HER CAKE AND EAT IT TOO!

SLAP!

23

27

GAULS, SINCE YOU HAVE SWORN TO GET RID OF ME, BY OSIRIS, I'LL SHOW YOU HOW A QUEEN CAN DIE!

NO, NO, BY TOUTATIS, LISTEN TO WHAT WE HAVE TO SAY FOR ONCE!!!

I'M SURE THAT CAKE'S NOT POISONED, I THINK IT LOOKS RATHER GOOD!

OH, YOU DO, DO YOU? VERY WELL THEN, LET THEM EAT CAKE!

SNAP!

THAT'S WHAT WE WERE ABOUT TO SUGGEST, O QUEEN...

THERE'S ONE OVER THERE.

OBELIX, DO YOU HAVE A REGULAR KNIFE OR A CAKE KNIFE?

MAY I?

CUT THREE PIECES OF THIS CAKE.

WITH MUCH PLEASURE!

HE SAID THREE PIECES, OBELIX!

WELL, I HAVE CUT THREE PIECES, HAVEN'T I?

YOU LITTLE PIG!

THERE ARE ALMONDS IN HERE... SLURP!... YUM!... ALMONSH ARE DELISH!

SCRUNCH! SMACK! SCRUNCH!

SCRUNCH!

SCRUNCH! SCRUNCH!

SO, QUEEN! YOU CAN SEE THAT CAKE ISN'T POISONED!

THEN WHAT'S EATING MY TASTER?

OBELIX!

BUT THERE ARE STILL A FEW ALMONDS LEFT...

POF! POF!

SEND FOR THE TASTER! I'LL CURE HIM!

WHENEVER I WANT TO DO SOMETHING, MR. ASTERIX OBJECTS!!!

BECAUSE MR. OBELIX DOESN'T KNOW HOW TO BEHAVE IN FRONT OF A QUEEN!

DRINK THIS, TASTER, AND YOU'LL FEEL BETTER!

SO, IT'S OKAY TO BEAT THEM UP, BUT IT'S NOT OK TO EAT ALMONDS?

THERE'S A TIME FOR BEATING AND A TIME FOR EATING! IT'S JUST GOOD MANNERS!!!

GLUG, GLUG, GLUG

I FEEL BETTER ... MUCH BETTER ...

IN FACT I FEEL GREAT! I'M HUNGRY!

THAT CAKE HAD NOTHING TO DO WITH THE TASTER'S ILLNESS, O QUEEN. HE'S JUST GOT A DELICATE STOMACH FROM EATING TOO MUCH RICH FOOD!

I HAVE TREATED YOU INJUSTLY, O GAULS! YOU ARE FREE TO GO! AND I DISMISS THIS TASTER WHOSE STOMACH HAS CAUSED THE QUEEN OF QUEENS TO MAKE A MISTAKE!

THERE WAS ENOUGH POISON IN THAT CAKE TO WIPE OUT AN ENTIRE COHORT OF LEGIONARIES. IT'S A GOOD THING WE DRANK MY ANTIDOTE.

SAY, THERE! THANK YOU SO MUCH! TO BE A TASTER IS MOST DISTASTEFUL ... IT WAS POISONING MY LIFE!

I HATE TO EAT AND RUN, BUT ... NOW IT'S TIME FOR MY SNACK.

LET'S GET BACK TO THE BUILDING SITE. WE'VE GOT TO FIND OUT WHO'S BEHIND THIS CRIME!

WHAT'S AN ANTIDOTE, ASTERIX?

AND AT THE WORKSITE ...

DOGMATIX! YOU NEARLY RAN ME DOWN!

THANK RA YOU'VE RETURNED! MY MASTER METROPOLIS DISAPPEARED JUST AFTER YOU WERE ARRESTED!

!!!

32

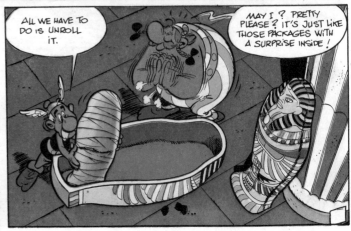

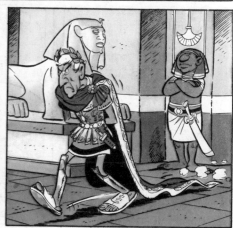

35

35

THE NEXT DAY, BY THE DAWN'S EARLY LIGHT...

COCK-A-DOODLE-DOO

SOON AFTERWARDS, AT THE BUILDING SITE...

MASTER! MASTER! COME AND SEE! STRANGE THINGS ARE HAPPENING!!!

WHAT'S GOING ON PAPYRIS?

ZZZZZ ZZZ

ZZZZZ

THE WORKERS HAVEN'T ARRIVED ON THE SITE. THERE'S NO ONE HERE BUT OUR PRISONERS MYNEMESIS AND PROBOSCIS.

?!?

GO AND GET THE DAILY NEWS!

YES, MASTER!

SOON AFTERWARDS...

THE BUILDING SITE IS SURROUNDED BY ROMAN LEGIONARIES! THEY WON'T LET OUR WORKERS IN!

IN THE NAME OF CAESAR! WE HEAR SOME GAULISH AGITATORS ARE HIDING ON THIS BUILDING SITE! WE ORDER THEM TO SURRENDER, OR WE'LL ATTACK!

?!?

WE ARE HERE AT CLEOPATRA'S BIDDING AND WE'RE NOT LEAVING TILL THE JOB IS FINISHED, BY TOUTATIS!

YOU'LL REGRET THIS, BY JUPITER!

NOW WHAT DO WE DO, BY ISIS?

WE BUILD FORTIFICATIONS, BY BELENOS!

YOU'RE RIGHT, BY BELISAMA!

ISN'T IT JUST ABOUT TIME TO LEAVE, BY ANY CHANCE?

34

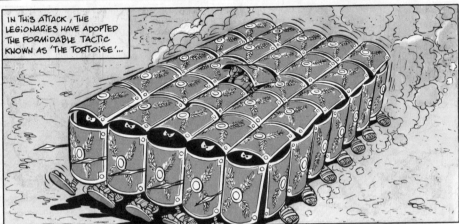

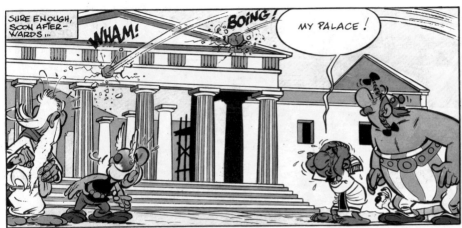

41

LOOK OUT! ONE OF THE BESIEGED MEN IS TRYING TO GET OUT!

WHOOSH!

READY?

READY!

THUMP!

BOING!

HE WENT THE SAME WAY HE CAME ···

JUST PASSING THROUGH ···

SOON AFTERWARDS, IN CLEOPATRA'S PALACE...

YOU REQUESTED TO SEE ME, O GAUL!

YES, O CLEOPATRA. MY LITTLE DOG HAS A MESSAGE FOR YOU.

HE'S SO CUTE ... BRING A BONE FOR THIS LITTLE DOG!

THIS SIMPLY WILL NOT DO! JULIUS CAESAR ISN'T PLAYING FAIR, BY ISIS! YOU MAY GO, GAUL! I'LL SEE TO THIS, BY AMMON AND BY HELIOS!

SCRRUUNCH! SCRRUUNCH! SCRRUNCH!

CALM DOWN, DOGMATIX... WAIT TILL THE QUEEN'S NEW TASTER HAS FINISHED TASTING YOUR BONE.

GRRRRR!

43

ER ... QUEEN ...
MY DEAR QUEEN ...

DON'T YOU QUEEN ME !!! WHEN I HEARD WHAT WAS HAPPENING, I RAN FROM THE PALACE WITHOUT EVEN STOPPING TO CHANGE MY CLOTHES !

OOPS!

WHEN YOU MAKE A BET, YOU MUST PLAY FAIR AND I HAD A RIGHT TO CALL UPON THE GAULS AND I'LL PROVE TO YOU THAT EGYPTIANS CAN BUILD BEAUTIFUL PALACES ...

... AND I DEMAND THAT THE ROMANS LET THE BUILDERS ALONE AND REPAIR ANY DAMAGE THEY'VE DONE BEFORE LEAVING. IT'S A SCANDAL ... AND...

... AND...

ALL RIGHT, ALL RIGHT ALREADY! I'M SORRY! I'LL DO ANYTHING YOU WANT ...

BIM !
BOOM !
TANTANTARAAA !

PFFFF

SO ... ER ... NOW WHAT DO WE DO ?

WE LIFT THE SIEGE AND REPAIR THE DAMAGE YOU'VE DONE, DUMBBELL !!!

AVE !

AFTER ALL, I WOULDN'T WANT CLEOPATRA TO SNUB HER NOSE AT ME !

SUCH A LOVELY NOSE, IN CASE WE FAILED TO MENTION IT EARLIER ...

LOOK! THE ROMANS ARE LIFTING THE SIEGE, BY BELENOS !!!

VICTORY, BY TOUTATIS !

AND IT'S ALL THANKS TO WHO ?

46

LATER, IN CLEO-PATRAS PALACE...

WE'VE FINISHED OUR WORK AND HAVE COME TO SAY GOOD-BYE, O QUEEN!

THAT NOSE...

YOU HAVE DONE WONDERS, GAULS, AND YOU ARE ENTITLED TO ALL THE GRATITUDE OF THE QUEEN OF QUEENS! ME.

I AM BESTOWING UPON YOU THESE PRECIOUS MANUSCRIPTS FROM MY LIBRARY IN ALEXANDRIA, O DRUID...

YOUR HIGHNOSE... ER... YOUR HIGHNESS IS TOO GENEROUS, BY BELENOS...

WHAT A NOSE!

IT SEEMS VERY LITTLE FOR ALL THE HELP YOU HAVE GIVEN ME. HOW CAN I EVER THANK YOU...

ALWAYS AT YOUR SERVICE... AND IF YOU EVER HAVE A MIND TO UNDERTAKE ANY OTHER ENGINEERING FEATS IN EGYPT, SAY A CANAL BETWEEN THE RED SEA AND THE MEDITERRANEAN...

JUST CALL ON SOMEONE FROM OUR COUNTRY, BY TOUTATIS!...

SOON AFTERWARDS...

IT SURE IS NICE OF CLEOPATRA TO LEND US HER PERSONAL BARGE TO TAKE US BACK TO GAUL...

...AND THE CAPTAIN GIVES THE ORDER TO SET SAIL...

DING! DING!

DING!... DING!

*FULL SPEED AHEAD!

BOOM!

DO YOU THINK WE'LL MEET THOSE PIRATES AGAIN, ASTERIX?

I DON'T KNOW, OBELIX, BUT I HAVE A HUNCH THEY'RE NOT FAR OFF!

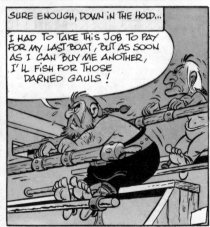

SURE ENOUGH, DOWN IN THE HOLD...

I HAD TO TAKE THIS JOB TO PAY FOR MY LAST BOAT, BUT AS SOON AS I CAN BUY ME ANOTHER, I'LL FISH FOR THOSE DARNED GAULS!

AFTER SEVERAL WEEKS OF A LUXURY CRUISE...

SCRUNCH SCRUNCH.

AT LAST THEY SIGHT...

A SHIP! A SHIP!!! ASTERIX, OBELIX AND MAGIGIMMIX ARE BACK!

THE GAULISH VILLAGE WELCOMES ITS HEROES WITH ITS USUAL ENTHUSIASM AND FEASTING...

... AND WE OWE EVERYTHING TO DOGMATIX!

A NOSE, MY DEAR MAN... WHAT A NOSE!

I SHALL NOW ARRANGE A LITTLE SONG...

AND FOR THE NEXT FEW DAYS, EVERYONE IS HAPPY... WELL, ALMOST EVERYONE...

NO OBELIX, NO!

I DON'T LIKE THE FORM OF YOUR NEW MENHIRS... LET'S KEEP THEM GAULISH!

THE END